THE
BEAR

Raymond Briggs

SCHOLASTIC INC.
New York Toronto London Auckland Sydney

ISBN 0-590-53523-4

Copyright © 1994 by Raymond Briggs.
All rights reserved. Published by Scholastic Inc.,
555 Broadway, New York, NY 10012,
by arrangement with Random House, Inc.

12 11 10 9 8 7 6 5 4 3 2 1   5 6 7 8 9/9 0/0

Printed in Hong Kong

First Scholastic printing, November 1995

Goodnight, Tilly. Here's Teddy. He'll guard you and keep you safe all night.

He's a wise old bear, isn't he?

Yes, Teddy knows everything.

Goodnight, Mummy...

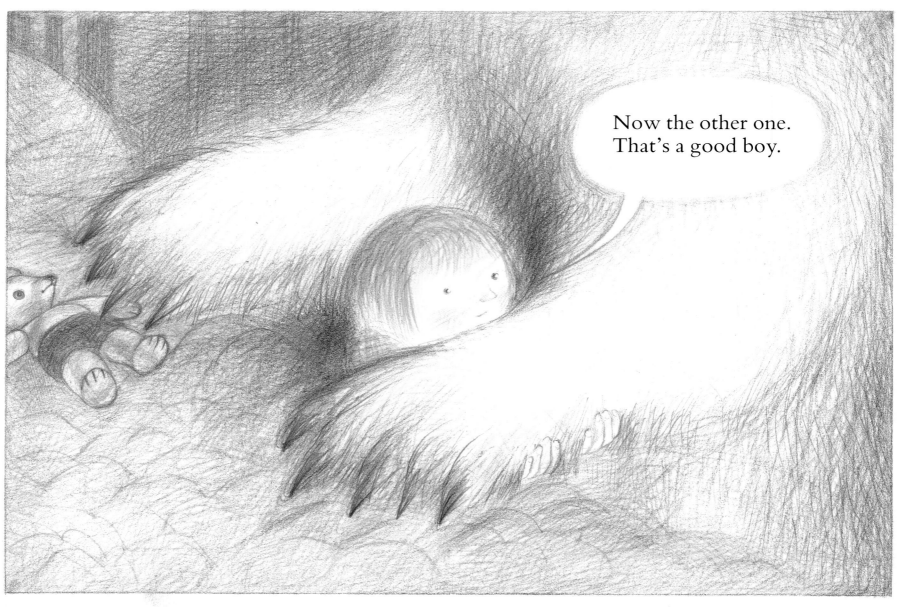

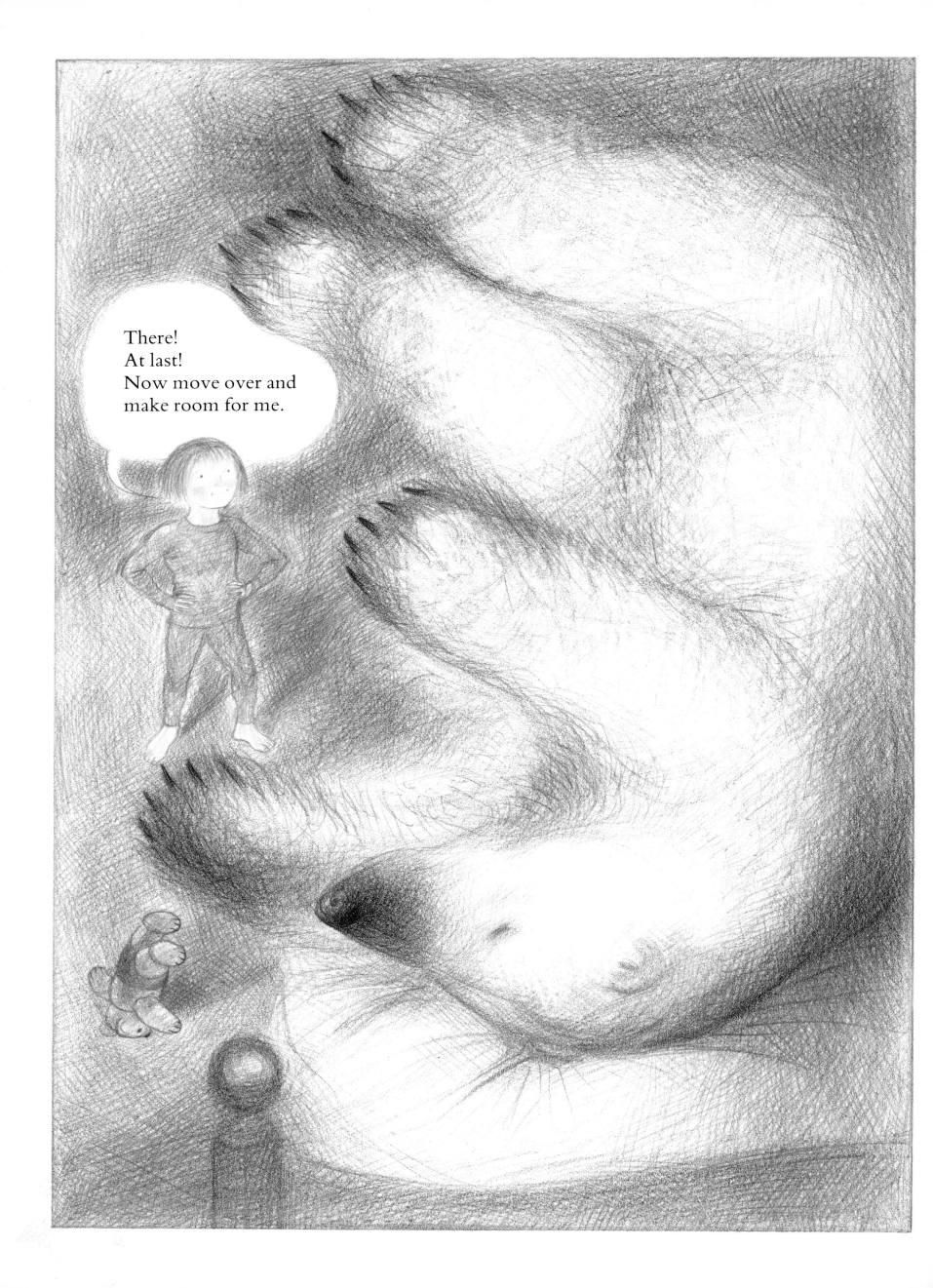

Oooh, Bear!
You're so *warm*!
Won't Mummy be surprised when
she finds us in bed together?

Mummy! Mummy! Daddy!
I was woken up by a bear!

    Oh? What a surprise.
    Was he a nice bear?

He licked my face with his tongue to wake me up.

    Did he?

It was ever so rough.
And he had great big black wet nostrils
blowing hot air in my face.

    Tilly! That's not very nice.

It's true!
He wanted to be friendly.   Well, mind you're friendly back.

You should see his teeth!
They're all yellow and enormous.
Longer than my fingers.
He's got real fangs.
I saw them when he yawned.
And his claws!
They're all black and curved like hooks.
He could easily tear me to bits
and eat me.

    Tilly!
    For goodness' sake!

He wouldn't though.
'He really likes me. I can tell.

I'll take him up a bit
of bread and butter.

Aaah!
The wonderful world
of a child's imagination.

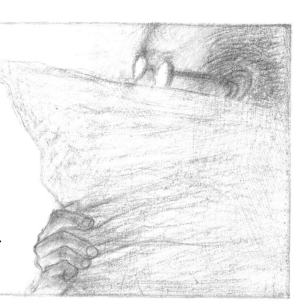

He's asleep now.
I've covered him up
with my quilt.

Did he like the bread
and butter?

He just licked it up with one flick.
You should see his tongue!
It's all black and about a foot long.

Ugh! Tilly!

Can he stay, Mummy?

Stay?
Yes, of course.
He can have
the spare bedroom.

No, I want him to sleep
with me.

Won't he roll over and squash
you in the night?

No, he'll just cuddle me.
I won't need a quilt.
He's the cuddliest thing
in the whole world.

Oh?
What about me?

You've got no *fur*, Daddy.
But you're *quite* nice.
I do still like you a *little* bit.

Oh, good.
I know I can't compete
with a bear.

Now you will be all right, won't you, Tilly?

Yes, Mummy.

Daddy is in his workshop,
but try not to bother him too often.

Yes, Mummy.
Don't fuss.
I've got the bear to guard me.

Yes, of course.
I really must dash.

Can I get extra milk from the milkman,
for the bear?

What?
Oh yes, of course.
Get as much as you like.
Byebye, Tilly.
Be good.

Byebye, Mummy.

You will make your bed, won't you?

I can't.
The bear is still in it.

Oh yes, well –
Never mind then –
Bye!

Hello, young lady.

Hello.
Can I have some extra
milk, please?
I've got a bear staying.

A bear, eh?
You'll need a lot
of extra milk
for a bear.
Is it a big bear?

Enormous.

Well . . .
Twenty pints, then?

I think one extra
will be sufficient,
thank you.

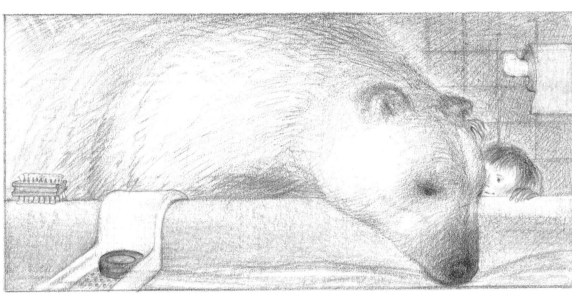

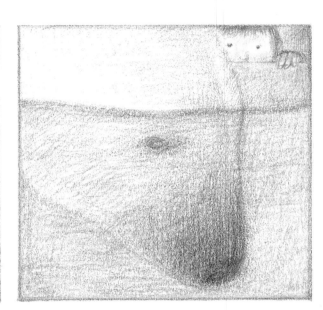

You silly bear.
You've soaked me *again*.

I'll dry us
in the
kitchen.

You do cause
a lot of work,
Bear.

Is it true bears like honey?
Try some.
It's Daddy's very own.

My!
You are quick.
It's all gone.
You are a greedy pig, Bear.

Bear! Bear!

Where are you?

How can you disappear when you're so big?

OH NO!

What are you up to, Tilly?

The bear's
done a poo.
I'm burying it.

Oh, I see.
Good girl.

Oh, there you are at last.
You're a very naughty bear,
making messes.

BAD
BOY!

DON'T!

Now I've got to go
and wash again.
Don't disappear.
Wait here.

Oh, you BEAST!
You've weed on the floor!

Horrible! Horrible!
Horrible!

You are *awful*!
I *hate* you.
Don't you dare do it again.

I'm going upstairs to have
a long think about what to do
with you, Bear. So wait here.

Look, Bear, I've decided you and
I have got to have a serious talk.
Come and sit down properly.

Now listen.
You know Mummy said you could have
the spare bedroom?
Well, she's never once seen you
and she may change her mind when
she finds out how big you are.
And if you are going to do poos and wees
all over the house, she'll *never* let you stay.
Mummy and Daddy mustn't see you
or they might put you out.
Do you understand?

Will you pay attention
when I'm talking to you!

Oh, you're *hopeless*!
You're always yawning
and falling asleep.

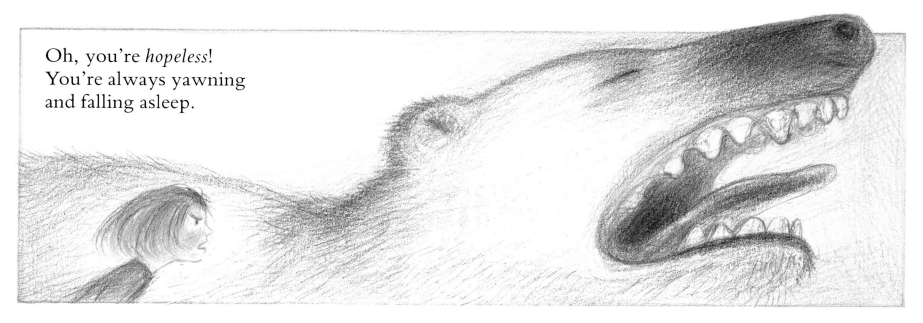

WAKE UP!
WAKE UP!

Come with me, Bear.

I'm going to put you in the spare bedroom.

No! *Left* here, stupid.

Up the stairs you go. Giddy up!

Now, you can *hide* in there, but remember you're going to sleep with me.

NO! Not in here! It's Mummy and Daddy's bedroom.

Bear! Bear! You can't hide *there*!

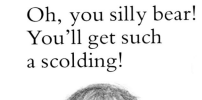

Oh, you silly bear! You'll get such a scolding!

Hello, Tilly!
Like something to eat?

Yes, please, I'm starving.
The bear is a lot of work, Daddy.

Is he settling in?

Yes, he's fast asleep in your bed.

Oh, good.
Will he sleep in between me and Mummy?

No. He's going to sleep with me.
You mustn't go in, you'll wake him up.

All right.
I'll go about on tiptoe
and we'll talk in whispers.

Hello,
Tilly!

Mummy!

Have you been all right?
Has the bear been looking
after you?

Sssh!

What?

Sssh! He's asleep.
In our bed.

Who is?

The bear. Sssh!
Mustn't go in
our bedroom.
Sssh!

Oh, I see.
Sssh!
We must whisper.

Yes. Sssh!

He's so big and quiet, Mummy.
He's the silentest thing I've ever known.
He's like a great big white ghost.

   Is he? He sounds like
   a polar bear.

I can't even hear him breathing
except when he cuddles me.
Then I can hear his heart beating,
too. His heart goes ever so slow –
it goes BOOM… ages ages ages
BOOM… ages ages ages BOOM,
like that.

   Well, I never. He's a long way
   from home, isn't he?

No, he's going to live here with me.
His fur is terrifically thick and
when I bury my nose in it,
it's ever so smelly, too.

   Oh Tilly, really!

No, it's a lovely smell.
All dark and smoky.

The bear is very good at hiding, Daddy.
Sometimes I look all over the house
and I can't find him.

But you say he is enormous?

He is, but he just seems to vanish like magic.
He could be in this room now
and you'd never know.

Golly!
Just imagine a great
big bear in here now!
I feel quite frightened.

Goodnight, darling.

Goodnight, Mummy.

Goodnight, Teddy.

There!

Now Tilly, whatever have you been
up to in our bedroom?

Oh, that wasn't me, Mummy.
That was the bear.

Well, the bear should have
tidied up, then.

I did scold him.
I expect that's why he's hiding
under the bed. He's sulking.

Is he there now?

Yes, of course he is.

Shall I give him a
goodnight kiss, too?

No, better not.
I think he's asleep.

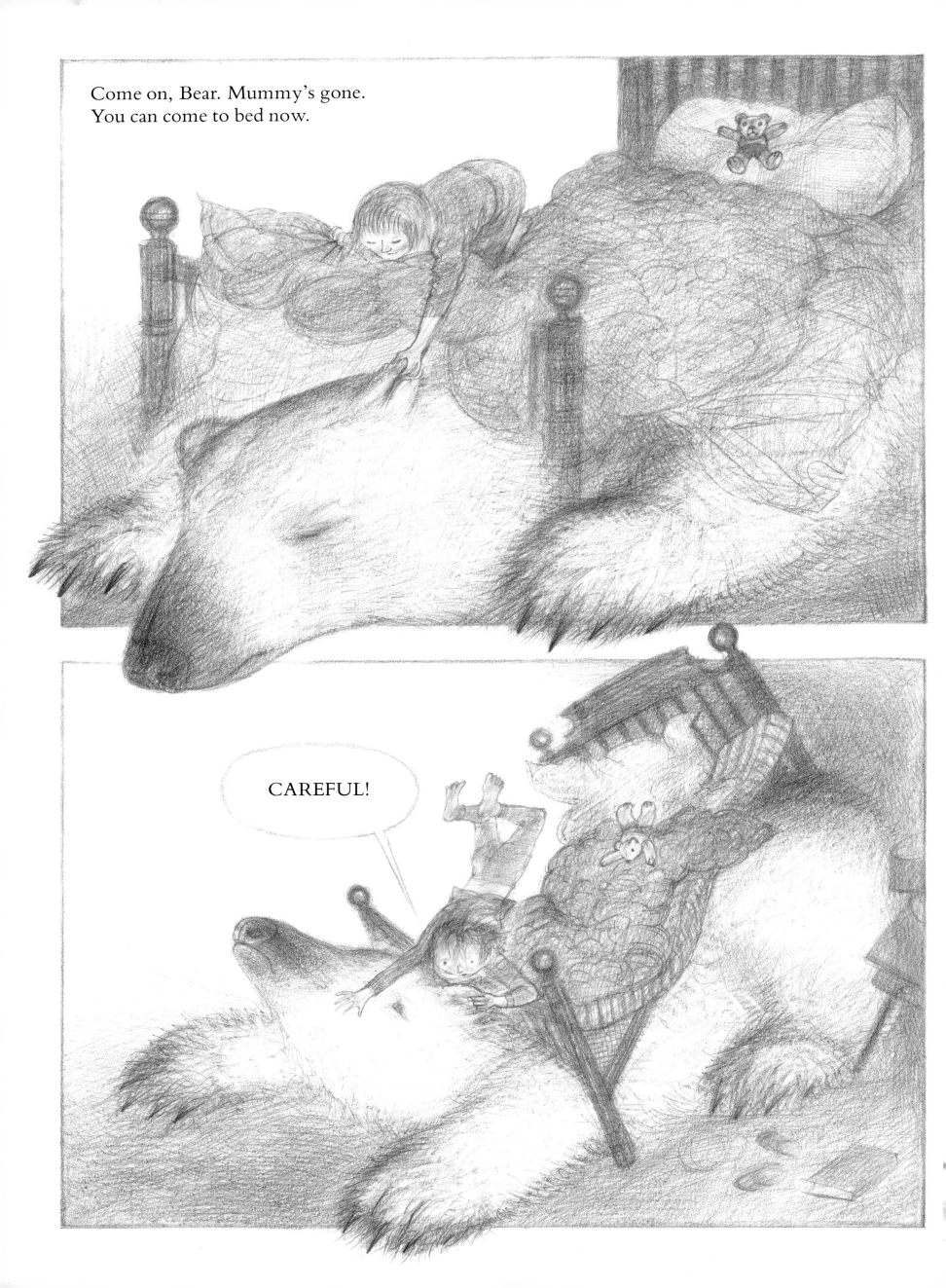

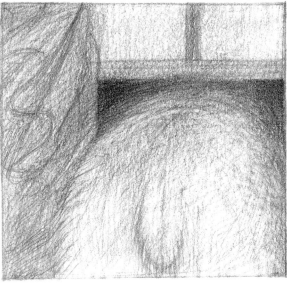

Tilly! Whatever's the matter?
He's gone!
He's gone!

Who?

The bear! He's gone!

Never mind, Tilly, sweetheart.
Don't cry, darling.
Bears can't live in houses
with people, can they, Teddy?
That sort of thing only
happens in story books.
Look Tilly, Teddy's nodding.
And he knows all
about bears,
don't you, Teddy?

Yes.
Teddy knows
everything.